ॐ

श्री ગણેશાય નમ :

श्री સરસ્વત્યૈ નમ:

ॐ ભૂર્ભુવઃસ્વ: તત્સ વિતુર્વરેણ્યમ ભર્ગો દેવસ્ય ધીમહી ધીયોયો ન: પ્રચોદયાત ‖

ECHOES OF THE SONGS FROM THE VALLEY OF HEART

TEARS FROZEN IN TO THE PROSE

By

SHAILESH ANANTRAI TRIVEDI

© (2023) SHAILESH ANANTRAI TRIVEDI

Attribute for the Cover page and Art work to
NIRUPAMA TANK MOGA

NOTION PRESS PUBLISHING PLATFORM

PAPERBACK ISBN NO. 979-8899063695

HARDCOVER ISBN NO. 979-8899063701

ॐ

श्री ગણેશાય નમ :

श्री સરસ્વત્યૈ નમ:

ॐ ભૂર્ભુવ:સ્વ: તત્સ વિતુર્વરેણ્યમ ભર્ગો દેવસ્ય ધીમહી ધીયોયો ન: પ્રચોદયાત //

The work is dedicated to
With love and respect- at the foot steps of ...

My Grand Parents
Durgashankar Chatrabhuj Trivedi
Jamunaben Durgashankar Trivedi
My Maternal Grand Parents
Harilal Jadavji Upadhyay
Maglaben Harilal Upadhyay
My Parents
Ananatrai Durgashankar Trivedi
Vijyaben Anantrai Trivedi
To My Elder brother
Late Dr. Ketan Anantrai Trivedi
To My Respected Teachers Of Mathematics At kamani
Forward High School Amreli
Shri Chimanbhai N. Joshi
Shri Bhupatbhai R. Joshi
Shri Rameshbhai M. Joshi

ECHOES OF THE SONGS
FROM THE VALLEY OF HEART

Music is the language without words,
Language is having words the pronunciation of which is not as
per the musical notes.
Still their fusion enriches another one to its full potential.
The pearls in the form of deep meaning of words hidden in oyster
of poetry cannot be found unless you deep dive in to the ocean of
music.
And the transcendental power of music cannot be felt unless you
sail the sea of music in the boat of words of poetry.
The true meaning of the poetry revealed only in the echoes of the
music of the songs in the valley of heart at the end when silence
prevails.

TEARS FROZEN IN TO THE PROSE

Tears are like precious gems stored deep in to the treasure of the
heart, they are taken out of the treasure on the most auspicious
occasions of the life.

PREFACE

I am not a linguist, a lyricist, or nor a laureate. Still I prefer to write.

In order to help someone who is having similar feelings to that of mine , but having no words to express them.

In hope, it may further help someone others, also in recognizing their own feelings, about which they themselves are ignorant due to lack of words.

I am thankful to all the authors and poets- who created those inspiring and beautiful literature-which I have read since childhood to this time- for their inspiring and amazing literary work. There, beautiful, amazing, hard work is always serving, as a light house for the seekers of knowledge. It also helps to those who seeks and admire beauty of words. Their work through which, I have gone through and inspired to humbly walk on their footsteps. Their painstaking efforts to awaken the readers are always a source of inspiration for all who love to read and write.

I am thankful to Notion Press publishing platform, Flipkart platform, Amazon Platform and all other publishers who have helped me in publishing the present work.

I am very much thankful and indebted for artwork for the cover page and other artwork to Ms. Nirupama Tank Moga (_Email-niruart13@gmail.com_).Her   artwork   is   deeply acknowledged herewith.

I am thankful to all my grandparents, parents, family members, relatives, friends, respected teachers, fellow students, fellow professors, colleagues, students, neighbors. I am also *thankful to all those who are with name or without name whose cooperation, blessings and well wishes inspires me to write this book and made this work possible.*

SHAILESH ANANTRAI TRIVEDI
Associate Professor
Civil Engineering
Vishwakarma Government Engineering College
Chandkheda-Ahmedabad
Gujarat-India
Email :: trivedisa12345@gmail.com

INDEX

PREFACE 5

INDEX 7

*CHAPTER-1 **TEARS FROZEN IN TO THE PROSE* 8

* CHAPTER-2 **PONDERING ON LIFE* 13

*CHAPTER-3**THE EDUCATION* 34

*CHAPTER-4 :** THE RELIGION SCIENCE AND MATHEMATICS* 55

*CHAPTER-5**THE PATH THAT READER FOLLOWS* ...73

*CHAPTER-1 *
TEARS FROZEN IN TO THE PROSE

1.1* I WAS AMONG THEM SOME WHERE SOME TIME*

As the life arrives in its mid stream; when I see;
An Ignorant and innocent boy;
Ignorant to the unfathomable world of learning;
Innocent to learn affections rather intelligence;
Climbing the steps of the school for the first time with tears in to the eyes.
And when I see ;
An Ignorant and Innocent youth coming-out of his study ;
Ignorant of what the society is ;
And Innocent to go for straight forwardness rather cleverness;
Struggle hard to hold his foot steady in the society with tearful eyes.
And when I see;
Ignorant and Innocent bride and groom ;
Ignorant to the true meaning of love and marriage ;
And innocent to believe love is stronger than harsh realities of what the life is ;
When bride with tearful eyes and groom walking the gentle step of sacred ritual of marriage ceremony encircling the sacred fire.
That lead them to an unknown dimension of life, society and world.
And when later in life the couple blessed with their first child and when they listen the first cry of the infant baby tear comes in to their eyes.

*And when the couple holds their baby for the first time in their
united hands together with tearful eyes and thanks to the God for
the gift of newly arrived child which has transformed the
marriage in true bond of love .*
And in journey of life when I see them all.
Tears too comes to my eyes;
As I was one among them somewhere some time.

✳✳✳

1.2*TEARS ARE LIKE PRECIOUS GEMS*

*Tears are like precious gems stored deep in to the treasure of the
heart, they are taken out of the treasure on the most auspicious
occasions of the life.*

✳✳✳

1.3*THE BOND OF THE FEELING*

*The bond of the feelings and love is much stronger among those
who have shared moments of tears together than among, those
who have shared only the moments of laughter together.*

✳✳✳

1.4*IN THE JOURNEY OF LIFE*

*When you have spent long memorable time with joy and cheer
together with your fellow human beings of the caravan you
belong.*
And when destiny separates your path from the path of them;
*At the cross road of life when you gaze the caravan you belong for
the last time;*
*The presence of tears in the eyes on either side transform the time
you spent together in to a precious gem.*
To be stored deep in to heart;

9

And in some future time; in solitary moments of life when you check that weather the gem stored deep in to the treasure of the heart is still there or not ?

And when you find it again, tears too come to the eyes again,pondering deep in to memory of joyous moments spent together with them.

It is a deep secret of our humane life is that tears and laughter's are not two separate things. But they are the summit and sag of our waves of feelings.

That is why in the happiest moments of our life tears come to our eyes.

And in our moments of deep sorrow when we cry by heart after some moments, a Mysterious smile emerges on our lips.

****

1.5*SUCCESS WHICH BRINGS TEARS IN EYES*

The success which brings tears in the eyes are often much worthy and admirable than the success which brings smile on lips.

****

1.6* TEARS IN EYES SOMETIME*

If some time, your eyes immersed in tears. It is an indication that society has not succeeded in seasoning of your heart ; and you have succeeded in preserving a child within your being .

****

1.7.*TEARS ARE THE ALPHABET OF LANGUAGE KNOWN TO GOD*

Tears are the alphabet of wordless language which God imparts to every infant who arrives in the world from heaven. It accompanies him for the rest of life. When the words become too incompetent to express the feelings, tears immersed to eyes.

10

Tears are the alphabets of only language known to God. All the rest of languages are understandable by man only.

***

1.8* AMAZING GIFT*

God gifted every human being with two amazing gift to heal the wounds of our brain induced by injuries from the sentimental trauma.
These are tears and dreams.
We seldom recognize and rarely notice its true significance.

***

1.9* CHILD TEARS AND GOD*

Child knows the only language of tears and does not know any of our spoken languages.
God too know the only language of tears and does not know any of our spoken languages.
And that is why the wordless prayers of child in the forms of tears are answered by the God in the form of mother.
And our similar selfless, wordless prayers like child in tears for the others often answered by God.
While our mature prayers for ourselves articulated in sophisticated words often remain unanswered. Even- though the words of the prayers well understood by the others.

***

1.10*BITTER WORDS SPOKEN BY YOU*

Bitter words spoken by you towards a person to whom you really love and care are destined to transform in to tears.

11

***

1.11 *AT THE TIME OF PRAYER*

Pearls transformed from tear in compassion towards suffering and pain of others ; can be exchanged against gems of knowledge from the God at the time of prayer.

***

1.12* AT THE GATES OF HEAVEN*

The tears wiped out, from the eyes of other, when you were alive, get transformed in to the precious pearls, in the moments of death . And that is the only treasure allowed to be kept with, at the gates of heaven .

1.13*TEARS RELATION WITH KNOWLEDGE*

The relationship of knowledge with tears is deeper than the relationship with the words of knowledge...

***

1.14 *TEARS OF GOD*

In the Book of "Sand and Foam" -Khalil Gibran -wrote enigmatic quotation –
" There must be something strangely sacred in salt .It is in our tears and in the sea. "
It may perhaps be due to
"Waters of sea is filled by tears of God."
Human beings felt so much of suffering and pain in the life bringing few drops of tears in their eyes as they have only pain of their own ...
While God is compassionate to the pain of all living creature and that compassion transforms in to the tears of God which can fill the sea ...

* CHAPTER-2 *
PONDERING ON LIFE

2.1*CROSS ROAD OF LIFE*

Every moment awaits some change in life.
In absence of courage and knowledge of the right change we simply move forward.
The moment we gather courage and knowledge for the change.
The very moment becomes your crossroad of life.

***

2.2 *WHEN A CARAVAN IS MOVING FORWARD*

When a caravan is moving forward.
It is identified by those who walks in the front .
But it derives its inner strength from those ,
Who remains silent so that the voice of the others can be heard .
Who remains inconspicuous so that others can be seen.
Who remains behind in support and care for others.
The caravan moves ahead on the path traced by the footsteps of the one who knows this secret by heart.

***

2.3*SILLY MISTAKES*

Silly mistakes, typical characteristics, and notorious behavior of someone near and dear to us annoy us tease us and often we quarrel on it.

On the walks of life.

A time comes when we lost them .

Afterwards when we met someone doing the same things , we are not annoyed, nor we quarrel on it, instead our heart filled with loving memories .

***

2.4 *SUCCESS IS NOT A DISCOVERY*

Success is not a discovery, it cannot be achieved by copying the manner in which it was achieved by others.

It is an invention that can be achieved in your own unique way when you have a passion, commitment, and determination to carve your own destiny

***

2.5*LIFE IS A CONTINUOUS JOURNEY*

Life is a continuous journey.

Like a staircase without landing.

You can make any step a landing.

Look around you and enjoy pleasant moments.

Look up to those have climbed higher steps and take inspiration from them.

Look downstairs and look at those who are behind at lower steps have sympathy for them.

Introspect and meditate for a while.

And climbs next step ahead.

It still remains a continuous journey.

Some time life leads to a place where there is mountainous terrain and no steps.

Took a rope of faith in God.

Throw rope towards mountain, show little courage and tightly hold the rope.

In few moments you will find yourself on a plateau higher than you were.

***

2.6*SWEET AND LOVING MEMORIES*

Sweet and loving memories enjoyed with someone near and dear to us for which no photograph survived.
Can only be shared with whom those sweet and loving memories were enjoyed. On the walks of life when you lost them . Those loving moments becomes your only unique possessions to be pondered in melancholic solitary moments .
And it becomes your solace of life.

***

2.7*LOVE INVENETED IN MARRIAGE*

Love invented in marriage is far more deep and sublime compared to marriage invented in love.

***

2.8* GOD BLESSES DIVINE INNOCENCE*

God blesses divine innocence on the face of child ; in whom God believes they will remain child forever and will never grow clever

***

2.9* PLACE OF PILGRIMAGE*

An ordinary place visited by you in some remote past in accompany with your near and dear ones.
On the long walks of life a moment does come in life when you lost them. If you happen to visit the same place once again life after a long period of time .You would like to visit the place in the manner in which it was visited earlier .Your heart is filled with lots of loving memories of your near and near ones. Your

journey transformed in to homage and for you the very ordinary place becomes a place of pilgrimage.

✳✳✳

2.10 *MESSANGERS OF GOD*

In the journey of life it is easy to move forward on straight path.
When we arrive on cross road of life we feel our self puzzled and confused and we are not in position to select direction on our own.
We wait for a while in deep introspection for selecting the unknown path ahead.
In such moments of life. a stranger appears from unknown direction towards us. Stands behinds us and holds his supportive hand and compassionate words to us and encourage us to move forward.
He leads us on the new and unknown direction holding our hand. We simply follow him with trust and aspiring eyes.
After walking some time to offer words of thanks to that stranger who has shown us new direction we look back.
To our surprise as when we become able to walk on our own they simply disappear among fellow travelers.
Our heart is filled with feeling of gratitude towards him.
Those strangers who arrive in our life on cross-roads of life to show our path of destiny are no ordinary persons. They are the messengers of God.

✳✳✳

2.11*INNOCENCE OF CHILD*

No intelligence can surpass the innocence of child.

✳✳✳

2.12* DREAM OF LIFE*

If you believe you have a dream and it does not really appear in your dream, than the dream you pretend to believe it is yours. Is not really your dream. It is borrowed from somebody else's dream.

✳✳✳

2.13*HOPE OF LIVING ALIVE*

It is not wealth, fame or glory but the love of someone near and dear to you keep the flame and hope of living alive.

2.14*SWEET MEMORIES*

The ultimate destiny of all humane relationship, possessions, success and achievements is nothing but, get it transformed in to sweet and loving memories.

2.15* FESTIVALS*

Festivals reminds us about the fact of the life that in spite of so much pain and suffering in individuals life we can still enjoy and smile together.

✳✳✳

2.16* SUCCEDING IN LIFE*

Those who succeeded in life they were not in search of success,
Instead they first get themselves qualified for it.
They have faith and concern for some cause relating to humane society.
They have in their heart passion for that cause.
They work hard with persistence, dedication and commitment.
They were not deterred by loses, criticism and risk.

They consistently work silently for long time with remarkable patience.

Success arrived in their life, at some cross road.

That destined moment of success came to them in their life, as natural consequences of the qualities they possessed.

In the similar manner when you visit your home town after a long period of time and you met suddenly and recognize your known childhood friend at the corner of some cross road of your home town...but the seeds of recognition was planted long ago....

✸✸✸

2.17* THE PATH LEADING TO SUCCESS*

The path leading to success which is full of struggles and sufferings is sometime becomes more memorable than success itself.

The sweet memories of the path full of struggle leading towards to the success – becomes more pleasant than – the success itself. These memories remain in heart forever, as they are similar to the memories of a mother of the times of nurturing of her infant baby, with full of struggle but sweet.

✸✸✸

2.18*MOMENTS OF DEATH*

Moments of death of someone near and dear to us are the greatest learning moments of life lessons, which cannot be learnt otherwise in universities and libraries. It compel us to introspect deep in to our own being how shallow we are, how inhumane we are, how poor is our way of thinking, and how ignorant we are to value the thing which are worthless and undervalue what is real worth .

It compels us to examine the real significance and worth of name, fame, wealth and achievements, as if everything at end is going to vanish in mist and abyss.

Those who are the cursed one whose eyes immersed in tears of regret, in those moments for them the memories of regret becomes like a bar of prison cell for the rest of life.

Those who are the blessed one whose eyes immersed in tears of pure love in these moments for them the sweet and loving memories became their solace of life and become the source of inspiration for the rest of life, to move ahead on the path of life alone.

✻✷✻

2.19* MOMENTS OF REALISATION*

A moment of realization do come in life when you realize that whatever you have is because of the sacrifice and struggle of someone near and dear to you .

They sacrificed their own enjoyment,want and dreams .so that you can fulfill your own enjoyments, wants and dreams. They make their life hard in order to make your life easy.

At this moment your heat is filled with gratitude and you want to offer them thanks. But it is a sad reality of life that such a realization does come too late in life. By the time you have such a realization, they have left for heaven. And you can offer them only tears of sorrow and regret.

If you are truly blessed, you will find those someone near and dear to you alive with you in the moments of such realization. As they truly love you they do not expect anything in return. At the most you can offer them is the joyous accompaniment, kind words, tender care and sharing of sweet memories with tearful eyes.

On the long walks of life when that envoy sent for you by the God to shape your life, left for the heavens your heart is filled with fulfillment and eyes immersed with tears of pure love.

✳✳✳

2.20* THE BOAT AND SHORE*

The life is like a journey in a boat when you finishes one voyage after paddling against wind in rough seas and arrives on a shore of an unknown and destined island with no light house.

When you land your feet on wet sands of the shore and walks few steps in excitement to mark your foot prints.

The very shore gets transformed in to an another boat to be sailed in to yet an another rough seas and taking you to an another unknown destined and mysterious island. With different fellow travelers.

By the time when you find yourself in the midst of unfathomed water extended to horizon surroundings you. The foot prints marked on the island you left washed away in the next high tide.

You again start paddling the boat against the winds in the hope of finding a beam of light house. When your eyes are gazing beyond horizons you left amazed by the twinkling stars of the dark night.

✳✳✳

2.21* THE WISE AND OTHERWISE*

If you are not wise, you cannot succeed; unless you succeed you are not wise.

✳✳✳

2.22* THE SUCCESSFUL COMPLETION OF WORK*

The successful completion of work or enterprise is like taking out treasure from the bank locker. Which require two keys to be operated simultaneously one possessed by you and the another one by the authority.

The one key which you possesses is the dedicated efforts and the another one key is the blessings of God

✳✳✳

2.23* WALKING WITH FRIENDS*

On the path of life somewhere some time we have walked together as fellow traveler. we joined our journey as strangers and when we departed becomes friends, we may have walked together long ago but we share some common happy memories that we would like to recall it again and again.

Pondering of the sweet memories make life meaningful and inspires us to walk forward.

To become a friend means to have something common among us. Let us accept together that is what common and let us respect together that is not common.

By Laughing a lot with friends and afterwards seeing tears on the their eyes, we learns that laughter and tears are no two different things but they are deeply rooted in each other and one can not have only one of this two ; one must have both alternatively in life ...

Friends are not persons ... with whom we agree all the times but we disagree with respect . They may not be correct all the times still we support him . They may not fulfill our expectations all the time still we love them. We may not like some of his habits still we like to be in company with them. They may be wrong but we do not become harsh towards them. friends are the persons to whom we love and respect without knowing why we have such a feeling towards them. some time we simply needs their company in order to make the time we pass a memorable time for the rest of life ...

***

2.24*THE CARAVAN OF LIFE ROLLS

ON TERRAIN OF TIME*

The caravan of the life rolls on the terrain of the time, sometimes plane and sometimes undulating rocky terrain.

Good wishes and blessings of friends- fellow traveler on the path of life gives us strength to move our caravan of life in the unknown terrain.

When you grow in age it is like climbing a hill your vision gets increased but your respiration increases and you get thirsty.

It is good wishes of friends cool water by which thirst is satisfied. Their feelings are like cool breeze which calms respiration.

Walking with friends crystallizes the simple time of clock in to the loving memories of past

***

2.25* THE REAL JOY OF LIFE*

The real joy of life is not in acquiring possessions and achieving success, but it lies in sharing it with loved ones and dear ones.

***

2.26* CLIFF OF TIME*

When we are walking on mountainous high cliff, as cliff is visible, we become extra cautious, careful, precautious and walk every step slowly and watching and thinking situation of every moments so that we do not fall in the deep valley .

But we seldom realize that we are also walking on the high cliff of time every moment, as the cliff is invisible, we rarely become cautious and careful to take every step, after due thinking and care. Ignorant of invisible cliff of time we several time, fall in the deep valley of pains, sufferings, miseries and failures. ..

2.27* AMONG ALL THE FEELINGS*

Among all the feelings someone has; The feeling which is the; most inspirational, motivational and encouraging; and provides strength to work hard and to overcome struggling and sufferings, is the feeling in the heart of being loved and cared by the someone near and dear one...

***

2.28*THE KINGDOMS*

The kingdoms of tyrants and dictators based on the power of swords;
Expanded across the world; which was expected to last for thousands of years ;
Crumbled and collapsed in decades and centuries.
While the kingdoms of prophets and preachers based on kind, humble and compassionate words;
Spread hardly in a small province; expected to vanish within lifespan of the preacher;
Lasted for thousands of years.

***

2.29* LANGUAGE POETRY AND MUSIC*

Music is the language without words,
Language is having words the pronunciation of which is not as per the musical notes.
Still their fusion enriches another one to its full potential.
The pearls in the form of deep meaning of words hidden in oyster of poetry cannot be found unless you deep dive in to the ocean of music.
And the transcendental power of music cannot be felt unless you sail the sea of music in the boat of words of poetry.

The true meaning of the poetry revealed only in the echoes of the music of the songs in the valley of heart at the end when silence prevails

✱✱✱

2.30* WORLD AND DREAM, AWAKENING AND

SLEEP, BIRTH AND DEATH*

What we have lost in world we desire to find it in our dreams. What we have lost in dreams we may find out it in our real world. What we fear in world appears in our dreams.

What we fear in our dreams vanishes in our world when we awake. Sleep is the Gate to enter in dreams from the real world it is also gate to exit from dream to real world.

From dreams when you awake through sleep you cannot remember your dreams properly.

From dreams when you awake directly without transition of sleep you can remember your dreams thoroughly.

The most essential part of the sleep providing rest to your mind is the phase of your dream. Unless you dream in your sleep-the sleep remains incomplete and do not provide rest to your mind.

The real world is a dream of God. As God is only one, real world is one common dream for all of us. Shared by all of us in the same manner.

While our dreams are unique and only we can see it, it cannot be shared with anybody else.

Birth is the gate of entry in to real world -dream of God, Death is the gate of exit from real world-dream of God

Birth is heavenly awakening and Death is heavenly sleep. If we awaken to the world without transition of death we can remember our life as a dream and awaken to our soul and there is no rebirth, if we awaken through the transition of death in rebirth we cannot remember our life as a dream.

24

In rebirth we enter from one dream to the another dream of God, as per our deeds and desires.

***

2.31*IN THE WORLD OF MANAGEMENT AND ADMINSTRATION*

In the World Management and Administration, paper serves three apparent purpose-Communication, Information and a Record . In its essence it also serves three subtle purpose- as a Witness of a decision, an Affirmation of an Agreement and a Declaration of a Resolve.

In the small organizations where membership sustains for a long period of time and which are administered on the bases of love, respect and trust like a family, papers are not essential and are eliminated in administration.

But in a large public organization where membership changes frequently - they are administered on the bases of laws, rules and code of conduct, Papers are essential, Where in such organization too if love, respect and trust can be developed to the extent possible- papers cannot be fully eliminated, but can be reduced to a certain extent.

When you replace a paper by a digital content, it is a partially paperless administration and not an absolute paperless administration.

Too much and too less a paperwork always hamper the effective functionality of administration.

***

*2.32*THE INTERVALS OF THE PRESENT MOMENTS *

The past has the characteristics of being one-unique, known, unchangeable and without the possibility of choice.

The future has the characteristics of being many, possible, unknown, changeable and possibility of choice.

The subtle moments of the present, transform one from many, the unknown from known, the changeable from unchangeable, and the many-choice into one-choice.

Just as the interval of the present moments is subtle on the timeline, the distance of the distinction between many-one, unknown-known, unchangeable-changeable, selective-non-selective is subtle and therefore they can be seen together.

And when the interval of the present moments on the timeline is greater, the distance of the same distinction is greater and therefore the two cannot be seen together.

***

2.33*LIFE IS BEAUTIFUL*

As there are friends in it to walk with …
As there are memories in it to cherish …
As there are little words from the literature in it to cultivate …
And there are little numbers from Mathematics in it
to work on it …

***

2.34* OFFERING – DONATION*

When your hand is raised to offer or donate something, keep your eyes down, so that the recipient has not to hide the helplessness in his eyes from you.

And when someone else's hand is raised to offer or donate something to you, look at that hand carefully, so that you can recognize it when the same hand comes in front of you in the future for help …..

✻✻✻

2.35*OUR TODAYS PROBLEMS*

Our todays problems, are deeply rooted, in the our solutions, to the then problems of the
yester years ...
Our solutions, perhaps may be with good intention ;
But due to limited knowledge
 and poor insight;
After a long period of time it turns otherwise ...

✻✻✻

2.36*THE PLACE OF PILGRIMAGE*

When you visit a place — after a very long period of time — where you have planted seeds of your dreams of life and spent a long time in hard work and life, full of struggle ...
The very place where you have stayed - was then felt much live, much buzzing, much hectic and very much moving now seems to be transformed in calm and silent place. with your much amazement many newly created things have replaced old one. and many new faces have replaced faces to whom you can recognize. These changes are the carvings of time ...
You are amazed, surprised, and delighted to be there in the known place with new transformation. And you gaze in the crowd with a hope to recognize things and faces known to you, with deep feelings of loving memories and attachments ...
Your heart is filled with sweet memories of the time you have spent there...and you want to be there for some more time ...
When- once the visit is over and again you leave the very same place with a heavy heart and tearful eyes... The tears in your own eyes pay homage to your own life of struggle and hard work. Sweet memories resurfaced there becomes tribute to your own life

span you have spent there and the very visit does not remain a simple visit, it becomes a pilgrimage ...

✳✳✳

2.37* INNOCENT SENSE OF HUMOUR AND LAUGHTER *

Humour in its sublime and subtle essence is nothing but-acceptance of our own ignorance ...

Those who are innocent, beloved and chosen souls; accepts their own ignorance by heart at the time of prayer to God; God bestows and blesses them with innocent, deep and divine sense of humour. And for them humour- too become a way of worshiping God ...

✳✳✳

Laughter is nothing but the subtle recognition of ignorance you have.

So in order to enjoy laughter deeply by heart – You must recognise your own Ignorance.

Once you recognise the vanity of worldly matters and your own ignorance- you will take things lightly and with ease.

That will help you in enjoying the moments of laughter by heart...

✳✳✳

2.38*ELEMENTS OF A STORY*

Every story in order to add in it, mystery, charm and interest, it must have some elements of exaggeration, irrational, illogical and unethical...

And if everything in it so, it can not have message, morale and appeal to human mind. So, story needs also to have real, rational, logical and ethical elements too.

Hence An ideal story must have both the elements artistically interwoven.

The order in which when story turns from one element to another it left someone with great surprise and amazement ...
Life too is a story. This what is true for story is also true for life too
***

2.39*THE MOMENTS OF THE PRESENT TIME *

Where the stream of our thoughts merges with the ocean of the thoughts of the Supreme Being.
That confluence point where both thoughts merges into one point.
That very point is moments of the present time ...

2.40*INDECISION-DILEMMA *

When you come across a crossroads in life,
When you are indecisive or having dilemma in choosing a path, or are undecided,
then by contemplating, meditating, praying, and being patient, at some moment in the present, God may determine a better path for you out of that uncertainty, or may He make a decision for you ...

***

2.41*PHOTOGRAPH OR A PICTURE*

Look at the beautiful moments of life with such a concentration of eyes that there is no need to capture them in Photographs or pictures to remember them.. and enjoy the beautiful moments of life to the fullest in such a way that there is no desire to remember them..

***

2.42*LOOSING ESSENCE *

You will loose your essence of the quality of character of your being once you become aware that you are having that one

***

2.43*UNDERSTANDING OF A COMMON MAN*

If you are rich but to make small purchases during a journey, you first have to get exchange of your large amount of currency from a common man, then only you can make small purchases.

In the same way, even if you are a scholar, you have to seek the guidance and advice of a common man to understand how to do small and ordinary things. Only then you can do small and ordinary things with their help.

***

2.44*PRAYER*

Just by praying to God, it is not possible for everything to happen as per your prayers .

But by the grace of God, you get the inspiration to make the necessary efforts to make it possible.

And for that, the necessary determination, knowledge, strength, patience and passion develop within you.

***

2.45*THE DAWN OF KNOWLEDGE*

When you become engrossed in the glitter of the world and indulge in pleasures, then understand that you are drifting in the flow of a deep sleep dream.

And when you become engrossed in sorrow due to the sorrows of the world, then understand that the dawn of knowledge is now approaching.

***

2.46*SIMPLE UNDERSTANDING*

There are many problems in life that can be solved with simple understanding or simple intelligence.
But if you are talented or intelligent and have given up simplicity and ease, then you cannot find solutions to such problems.

***

2.47*STRUGGLE AND SUFFERING OBSERVED IN CHILDHOOD*

Struggle and suffering observed in childhood is not a curse .. As it imparts precious lessons of life which cannot be learnt otherwise .. And it becomes ones greatest strength when one grows .

***

2.48*PATH OF LIFE *

When you look back on your life and ponder through the treasure trove of memories..
Then you will find that you have found more happiness, peace, satisfaction and fulfillment on the path that God has chosen for you that you have accepted with faith, dedication and ease than on the path that you chose or wanted to choose with your own cleverness, cunningness and intelligence.

***

2.49*HAVING NO WORDS TO EXPRESS THEM*

I am not a linguist, a lyricist, or nor a laureate. Still I prefer to write.
In order to help someone who is having similar feelings to that of mine , but having no words to express them ..

In hope , it may further help someone others, also in recognizing their own feelings ,about which they themselves are ignorant due to lack of words.

****

2.50*MAXIMS OF LIFE *

(Note And Attribute- This Article 2.51 Maxims of Life is inspired by the some quotations from anonymous source. It is presented in its recalled revised and in expanded form. credit attributed of this article to the original anonymous author)

Be Humble In Success.
Be Introspective In Failure .
Be Merciful In Victory.
Be Resolute In Defeat.
Be Industrious In Poverty.
Be Generous In Wealth.
Be Polite In Authority.
Be Honest In Service.
Be Passionate In Study.
Be Silent In Anger.
Be United In Injustice.
Be Tolerant In Pain.
Be Sweet And Assertive In Talk.
Be Committed In Promises.
Be True In Relationships.
Be Empathetic In Love.
Be Devoted in Prayers.

****

*2.51*PEARL OF DESIRE*

A desire of yours is a pearl.
Time line is a string.

The actual realization of the desire is the stringing of pearls into a necklace.

When you hold pearls, in selfless manner and as an instrument of God, in your palms in a gesture of homage, with the intention of offering them to God... then the God readily accepts it for stringing it into a necklace... And thus that desire actually realized...

When you hold your pearls in your fists with ego and attachment... then the God cannot readily accept it and cannot take it for stringing it into a necklace... And thus that desire cannot actually realized...

****

2.52 INVOLVEMENT –NON INVOLVEMENT*

Just as in youth one becomes involved in worldly matters due to attachment...

Similarly, in old age one becomes non involved from worldly matters due to detachment.

****

*2.53*PRECEDING–SUBSEQUENT EVENT *

When a preceding event occurs, then a subsequent event occurs after it, so we believe that this event occurred first, and that the subsequent event occurred in its wake ...

But that is not the case in the design of fabric of existence – in it, the subsequent event that occurred was predetermined – the preceding event that occurred had to occur accordingly, and so it was...

*CHAPTER-3**
THE EDUCATION

3.1*CREATION OF ART*

During the creation of art if an artist in his total devotion lost his own identity and merely act as an instrument of God , then the created art becomes unique and heavenly masterpiece.

****

3.2* LESSONS FROM PRAYERS*

One of the important lessons of life we learn in school is prayer. That is because it gives us understanding of the purpose for what the rest of lessons stand for.

****

3.3*THE REASEARCH AND INNOVATION*

The research and innovation based on intuition, meditative introspection, insight,and presented with brevity is often more worthy, amazing and admirable compared to research based on extensive citation,multiple referencing and voluminous presentation.

****

3.4*FARMING OF TEAK WOOD*

Education is like a farming of teak wood; where you cannot have harvest at the end of every season.
If you work hard with patience and faith these are the same qualities which are essentially required in farming.

Finally when harvest arrives some day in life, it arrives with abundant pleasure and wealth.

****

3.5*READING*

Reading is

A journey of acquiring meanings of new and unknown words with the help of known words.

And acquiring new meanings of known words with the help of new and unknown words.

A realization of ignorance in our own understanding and understanding meaningfulness in what we believe as ignorance.

A transformation of feelings in to words and words in to feelings.

And a search of finding proper word for expressing our feelings, which we are unable to explain .

****

3.6*QUOTATIONS*

When we appreciate any quotation or sayings, it indicates that the inherent meaning of the quotation , was already known to you ; only words were missing , somebody else realized the same, has succeeded in carving your wordless understanding in to words .

****

3.7* IN THE WORLD OF LEARNING*

In the world of learning .
There are only two real subjects .
They are language and mathematics .
The first one helps us in expressing and communicating the beauty of hearts and the second one in expressing and communicating the beauty of brain.

35

They are the only true and prime subjects in essence.
The remaining subjects are merely offspring's of the former two.
Learn them thoroughly.
And you will learn the rest of the subjects very easily.

✽✽✽

3.8*TRANSLATION*

Every language has different and distinct glossary, thesaurus, syntax, stanza, verse, rhyme sayings and proverb. Its own specific way of pronunciation and melodious rhythm of liturgy and poetry. It imparts every language a unique identity.

Its unique identity cannot be imagined totally in the mirror of translation. You can have at the most faint glimpses of what it may look in its originality.

The translation of prose is like a color picture, and translation of poetry is like a black and white picture, of bouquets taken after night when flowers have withered and fragrances have gone. Sadly fragrances can never be captured.

In the case of second translation if it is carried out from another translation of its original. It seems like a negative image of its true picture of what a beautiful bouquet of flower was in its originality.

✽✽✽

3.9*UNDERSTANDING OF WHATEVER YOU HAVE LEARNT*

Understanding of whatever you have learnt remains incomplete unless you become able to teach it to others.

***

3.10* THE MASTER KEY OF UNDERSTANDING THE METHOD OF LEARNING*

The master key of understanding the method of learning of any new and unknown subject-matter is deep pondering on how you have learnt your own mother tongue.

That is because.

The very first thing any child learns in his life is nothing but the mother tongue.

The mother tongue is introduced to a child in its most beautiful form of music and singing of lullaby.

The essential elements present in which you learn mother tongue is the presence of persons who have already learnt it. Conducive environment its significance and correlation with life, imitation, repetition and pleasant learning.

All your early emotions and feelings are deeply attached to your mother tongue. Which you are emotional and want to express your deep feeling you naturally prefer to express in mother tongue.

And knowledge of mother tongue will accompany you for the rest of life.

Approach the new subject matter from its most beautiful side. Search the elements present in the learning of the mother tongue for new subject matter. and you will have pleasant journey of learning anything new and unknown to you.

***

3.11* THE CYCLE OF UNDERSTANDING AND LEARNING*

If you want to understand life learn language.
If you want to understand language learn society .

If you want to understand society learn nature.
If you want to understand nature learn Science.
If you want to understand Science learn Mathematics.
If you want to understand Mathematics learn music .
If you want to understand music learn sentiments .
If you want to understand sentiments learn compassion .
If you want to understand compassion learn soul.
If you want to understand soul learn scriptures.
If you want to understand scripture pray to God.
And if you are able to pray to God. Learning is not required.
If you are already praying to God with faith and devotion
It is not necessary to you to enter in to the cycle of understanding and learning.

***

3.12* SOUND OF RINGING BELL OF SCHOOL*

When a child consider and like the sound of ringing bell of school in morning at beginning of school he succeeds in literature, academics and research.

When a child consider and like the sound of ringing bell of school in evening at the end of school he succeeds in arts, sports and business.

When a child does not like sound of ringing bell of school he goes astray on the path of life.

Those who are unfortunate, who have not given any chance to listen the ringing sound of school bell, their life is lost in ignorance and misery.

***

3.13* THE NEW AND UNKNOWN LANGUAGE*

Every teaching and learning Endeavour in its ultimate essence is nothing but to learn a new and unknown language.

The new and unknown language is like a unique and distinct language spoken by inhabitants of an island. Those like cultivators and masters of some faculty of humane knowledge. Where the students are like strange travelers and teachers are like native translators.

∗∗∗

3.14* THE SUBLIME PARADOX*

Humane race has learned language by poetry, liturgy and musical melodies while script and grammar were invented later, but in school we start teaching language by script and grammar.
Humane race has learned Mathematics by perceiving mathematical truths by appreciating its beautiful patterns and symmetry. While theorems and proofs were invented later. But in school we start teaching mathematics by theories and proof.
This reverse direction of educating children compared to how humane race   has learned these subjects; is a sublime paradox. Where we are teaching those things first , the understanding of which can be attained at much later stage in life. And leaving those things not introduced which can be understood at much earliest stage of life; left to be explored on its own.

∗∗∗

3.15* KIND AND CARING WORDS*

Kind and caring words of a teacher lasts longer in student memory compared to words full of intelligence.

∗∗∗

3.16* TEACHING AND EDUCATIIING*

TEACHING	EDUCATING
Passes Instruction	*Evaluates Instruction*
Accumulation of Information	*Judging Significance of Instruction*

Ends in examination	Examining the life
Confined within curriculum	Curriculum unconfined
Within four walls	Within four directions
For possessing degrees	For possessing wisdom
For procuring wealth	For generating wealth
Dependent on book	Independent of book
Discipline oriented	Oriented to integrate discipline
Induce competition	Induce compassion
Enslaves thinking process	Freedom of thinking process
Conservative	Rationalist
Time bound	Life long
In school and universities	In nature and society
It moulds mind	It develops mind
Intellectual development	Character development
Marks and Grade oriented	Knowledge and wisdom oriented
Asks for obedience	Demands discipline
What is taught is to be respected as truth	Truth is required to be found
Teacher is teacher and student is student	Teacher and student learn together
Teacher is master	Teacher is guide
Student is a follower	Student is a fellow
One way talk	Two way talk
Develops successful personalities	Builds responsible citizens
Learning with tear and fear	Learning with joy and cheer

***

3.17* MAJOR ASPECTS OF ATTAINMENTS OF LEARNING*

INFORMATION	KNOWLEDGE	WISDOM
Collection and reception of data	Applications and modified presentation of data	Evaluating and significance of data
Summation of time and book needed	Summation of information and experimentation needed	Summation of knowledge and affection needed
Can be purchased by money	Simply money will not help self involvement needed	Money and time will not simply help it. Needs experiencing life with sentiments
A child can procure	A youth can achieve	Elders can reach
In words and symbols	In action and works	In deeds and steps
Latest will be praised	Current will be implemented	Old is Gold but new is to be respected
Answer what is ?	Answer how to ?	Answer why ?
Everybody can procure	Some of them can get	Few of them can attain
May be good or bad	Good information to be selected to procure knowledge	Only best and most useful will be utilized for attaining

		wisdom
Library is the custodian	*Schools and universities are the custodian*	*Nature and society are the custodian*
Can be given to anybody who can read and listen	*Can be given to those who have seen and experienced*	*Can be given to those who feels*
Can be used for many purposes	*Avoiding bad utilization of information*	*Best and true utilization*
Information may be in very large quantity	*Primary summarization and better analysis reduces its quantum*	*Optimum summarization and synthesis of information make it relatively small quantum*
Unnecessary and repeated information may be there	*Repetition avoided and necessary information utilized*	*Essence of information extracted*
Initial stage of learning process	*Intermediate stage of learning process*	*Ultimate stage of learning process*
Information is valuable when is being referred	*Knowledge is valuable when it is correctly used*	*Wisdom is valuable when it creates bond of love among people*
Reflects in talk	*Reflects in act*	*Reflects in step*
May be related to	*Mixed*	*Integrating*

particular field	*application of information from different fields*	*many facets of human life*
Can be remembered by repetition	*Can be achieved by coordinating various information*	*Can be achieved by heart and mind together*
Provide platform for learning and earning in life	*Provide success and satisfaction in life*	*Provide true meaning to life*
Dependent on others	*Partially dependent on others and partially depend on self*	*Mostly dependent on intuition and inspiration*
Can be achieved in short time period	*Can take much more time*	*Can be achieved after long time*
Communicating together	*Working together*	*Loving together*
Reply within the content of what has been told	*Reply beyond the content of what has not been told*	*Reply is exclusive beautiful and artistic*
Provide necessary infrastructure for getting knowledge	*Provide necessary infrastructure for attaining wisdom*	*Provide necessary infrastructure for better living*
Reception of words	*Speaking of words*	*Telling of words.*

****

3.18*TERRAIN OF EDUCATION*

Education is a strange and amazing terrain where the destinations are reached by the longest route and through rough terrain. While the destinations transformed in mirage in shortest route and through plain terrain.Blessed are the traveler who find the guide for themselves who show them longest route, through rough terrain to be followed and caution them to avoid short routes through plain terrain.

Those who choose for themselves the shortest route and plain terrain for them the destinations remain an illusion. Their journey becomes wandering and they reach nowhere.

✳✳✳

3.19* FEELING AND UNDERSTADNING*

We seldom understand the meaning of the words of prayer, still we feel ourselves showered with peace of mind and bliss.

This hints towards one subtle realities of life that life is more about feelings and less about understanding.

That is why in our early childhood we feel the enjoyment of the life too much when we understood too little.

✳✳✳

3.20* HABIT OF LEARNING NEW THING*

If you make a habit of something learning new always. You will never find yourself bored. And will never feel yourself that the meaningfulness in life is missing.And your heart will remain filled with joy and pleasure in admiration of beauty of newly acquired learning.

3.21* BIOGRAPHIES*

The study of biographies is the most beneficial and elevating study.

Still, surprisingly university curriculum often miss it.

***

3.22* THE ULTIMATE PURPOSE OF SEEKING KNOWLEDGE*

The ultimate purpose of seeking all knowledge and all philosophies is to provide solace and consolation to our suffering soul destined to vanish in trap of death.

3.23* NURTURING A DREAM TO BECOME A TEACHER*

If as a student on acquiring the understanding of the new content or subject matter , your heart is filled with sharing it with other fellow students around you. Then you are nurturing in your heart a dream to become a teacher one day.

3.24* MYSTERY OF HISTORY*

The moments of present times, are fragile and soon vanish in the whirlpool of time. The moments of future, are in mist nothing can be seen through. Only the moments of past are crystallized, stable and stationary.

And that is why the only direction available for exploring the knowledge to the seeker is past.

Hence the study of History is most beneficial and elevating for the seekers of knowledge.

As our own memory beyond certain time is always in mist and unknowable – similar is true for the whole mankind.

The knowledge of History, beyond certain time always remains mystery.

The exploration of the future is the secret key to unlock the mysterious past.

The Knowledge of past is the secret key to unlock the mysterious future.

The mystery of History is that past and future are deeply rooted in each other.

And the History of exploration of knowledge of mystery is that more and more you explore it more and more it will be amazing.

✹✹✹

3.25* UNIVERSITY WITHIN LIBRARY*

Library situated within the university, is easily noticed.

But, it is rarely noticed that, university is also situated within the library.

Libraries are not merely collection of books, but they are real open universities in its true sense.

Where no curriculum defined, but you can define it on your own.

Where there are no teachers, but you can become teacher of your own.

There are no exams at the end, as study gets never completed there.

No degrees offered there, but it imparts meaning and makes degree worthy that you already possess.

✹✹✹

3.26* SEVEN PRINCIPLES OF LEARNING*

There are seven principles of learning. The first one without hard work learning and gaining of knowledge is not possible. If you have understood the very first principal thoroughly by heart. It is not necessary to know the remaining six principles

✹✹✹

3.27* ROOT CAUSE OF IGNORANCE*

After learning reading and writing. All the remaining ignorance thereafter is having root cause in our idleness.

✳✳✳

3.28* TEACHERS ARE VOLUNTARILY DETAINED STUDENT*

Teachers are like voluntarily detained student, who preferred themselves to remain voluntarily detained student, for the rest of life, in order to help other students, to move forward in the next standard to pursue their study further ...

✳✳✳

3.29*A BOOK AND A TEACHER*

A Book is a teacher too...with vast and deep knowledge - But you cannot ask him questions, as they are distant to you in time and space...

A Teacher is a book too...with limited practical and workable knowledge -But you can ask them questions, as they are near to you in time and space ...

In the initial stage of learning when your mind is full with questions- and when you are not mature enough to walk alone - it is beneficial to approach   a kind and caring teacher, who can help you in opening doors of knowledge for you ... You are truly blessed if you find and met any such one ...

In the later stage of learning, when questions vanish - and when you become mature enough to walk alone -It is beneficial to approach a book penned by a learned and wise one, which can open doors of wisdom for you ...You are truly blessed if you find any such one...

✳✳✳

3.30*KNOWLEDGE *

Knowledge of anything means - at the same time - knowledge of its opposite too.

***

3.31*TEACHERS*

All those who have guided and supported to you on the path of life in one or other way at any juncture of life they becomes your respected teachers ...

***

3.32*INFORMATION*

*Information is like grapes; fresh they
are- better...*
Wisdom is like wine; aged (ancient) they are- better ...

***

3.33*IMITATION *

Imitation is the greatest tool of learning.
A child learns almost everything by imitation .
A pupil imitates his mother and teacher.
A student understands, partly by imitation and partly by, correlating his own experiences.
In the journey of imitating others , when some one becomes mature, he learns, what to imitate and what not to imitate .
Finally one learns how to follow, what his own heart is saying- and how to act accordingly his own intuition ....

***

3.34*THE THREE PLACES WHERE KNOWLEDGE IS HIDDEN ARE *

The wrinkles on the brains of the wise who have devotion for study and knowledge ...
The wrinkles on the faces of experienced old people ...
The wrinkles formed by spines of books in rows on the shelves of libraries ...

****

3.35*EVERY LEARINNG ENDS *

Every learning ends …
In order to
Make you
Competent to
Pursue some higher learning.

****

3.36*JOB OF A TEACHER*

Job of a teacher is to …
Simplify the subject to the students -So that students do not fear it;
Introduce beauty of the subject to the students -So that students love to study it ;
Persuade students to study sincerely and put efforts for hard work -so that students can understand that it is not an easy task;
Advice students to work with patient -so that student can understand that it is a long journey;
Educate students that the real purpose of the acquiring knowledge is for betterment, welfare and help of fellow human beings-So that students learns empathy and affection;
Develop self confidence among students -so that student can proceed the journey of knowledge on their own, can move alone and don't become dependent ;
Plant seeds of passion in the heart of students for seeking knowledge -so that the knowledge of the students surpass the knowledge of their own teachers…

$$***$$

3.37*READING*

Reading is the interpersonal and collective meditation to look inside the common soul of humanity

$$***$$

3.38*THREE S OF DESIGN*

Three S Of Creation and Imagination
Size (Dimensions, Measurements)
Shape (Form, Figure, Geometry)
Substance (Material)
Three S Of Requirement
Safety (Security, Protection)
Strength (Capacity, Competent, Soundness, Tough)
Splendid (Aesthetic, Look, Architecture)
Three S Of Purpose
Suitable (Function , Purpose, fit, appropriate)
Sustainable (Durable, Viable, maintainable)
Saving (Economic, Frugal, Conservation)

$$***$$

3.39*WHEN YOU SOLVE A DIFFICULT PROBLEM *

When you solve a difficult problem or any sum from any subject ... after working on it for much time. Often you have first reaction is that, how poor understanding you have- or how ignorant you were -so that you were not able to understand such a simple fact or truth... and it take too long time to realise it ...

$$***$$

3.40*DEVELOPMENT OF UNDERSTANDING*

Understanding among students develops with individuals own insight -Which is essentially intrinsic and implicit in nature.

Which does not develop in very organised manner and in short span. It flourishes in due course of time in organic manner.

The job of a teacher is to increase the potential and probability-for the development of such understanding among student .Which can be done by providing information and instruction normally in the form of language -which is essentially extrinsic and explicit in nature.

✱✱✱

3.41*INTENSIVE STUDY*

Unless you appreciate the beauty within;
Unless you recognize harmony and order within ;
Unless you know within- how worthy it is for human
life and society ;
Within the content you are assigned and going to study ;
You will not be able to love to study it.
Nor you will dedicate yourself for its intensive study…

✱✱✱

3.42*TEACHER (GURU) AND DISCIPLE *

It is not always the case that the disciple is in search of the Guru; it is also true that the Guru is also in search of the disciple..

Wherever they have reached in the journey of knowledge, the God unites the disciple with the guru who has already reached there. And to the Guru the disciple who have already reached there .

✱✱✱

3.43*MOTHER TONGUE*

Introspection on how you learned your mother tongue is the key to getting guidance on your own in learning any new subject.
Essential basic elements for learning mother tongue :

1. Continuous association with people who know and are familiar with that language.

2. Lively introduction to the flowing life, the surrounding environment and the words related to the necessities of life and their use.

3. The presence of a dedicated mother-like teacher to teach you.

4. Continuous repetition and intensive study of the alphabets by rote.

5. For the introduction of the language, the beauty of the language is introduced through musical and poetic expressions of the language and the instillation of love for the language.

6. Introduction and knowledge of the rules that connect words, i.e. the rules of grammar.

7. Introduction to the literature written by the writers who have reached the essence of the language and its guidance in the journey of life

8. Acquisition of the ability to understand the thoughts of others and express one's own thoughts and through this, the fulfillment of one's life's duties

These basic elements of the study of the mother tongue are that basic elements for the subject that you yourself need to identify for the new thing that you have to learn. only in this way can you move forward on the path of study on your own through introspection

****

3.44*ATTAINMENT OF KNOWLEDGE*

There are two ways to attain knowledge. First — In which you yourself try to attain knowledge but years and years pass on that path.

Second — In which God tries for you to attain knowledge, in that path, knowledge can be attained in a moment.

But before God tries for you to attain knowledge, He checks whether you have the passion and patience to walk on the path of attainment of knowledge for years and years.

***

3.45*TEACHER *

Whose past; that is your future; that is your Teacher (Guru)...

***

3.46*GOAL OF TEACHING *

One of the goals of teaching is to show the relationship between the most complex subject matter and the simplest subject matter .

***

3.47* LIBRARY TICKET*

When you enter in library, with library ticket, it becomes your gate pass for the city of knowledge ...
When you come out after a prolonged time, it becomes your highest educational qualification ..

***

* 3.48*THE JOURNEY OF EDUCATION *

Just as a small child, while trying to walk on a field path, holding his grandfather's finger, without any specific purpose or hope of achievement, tries to take steps with the simple faith that there must be some welfare or joy behind walking like this, and starts taking steps with enthusiasm and joy, and by walking like this, he becomes capable of taking steps on his own in that journey and moves forward ..
Similarly, if a student also tries to receive education in whatever lesson the teacher gives him on the journey of education, without any specific purpose or hope of achievement, with the simple faith that there must be some welfare or joy behind this lesson,

53

and starts studying with enthusiasm and joy, and by studying like this, he becomes capable of learning on his own in that journey of knowledge and moves forward ......

****

*3.49*GIVERS OF KNOWLEDGE*

Two intangible givers of knowledge are death and time
Two tangible givers of knowledge are Guru (Teacher, Master) and scripture
Two inherent givers of knowledge are Discourses Satsang and travel

CHAPTER-4 :
* THE RELIGION SCIENCE AND MATHEMATICS*

4.1* SCIENCE AND RELIGION*

Those who believe in science and neglect or have no faith in religion.

they should understand that, in school the prayers are placed before the period of science.

Those who believe only in religion they should understand that person who is suffering from hunger cannot be asked for prayer unless they are properly feed.

Science and religion are not two opposites but they are substitutes to each other. When they substitute each other they become blessings for the humane society, and when they oppose each other they cannot fulfill their intended purpose.

When science and religion are working in synergy, the peace, progress property and protection are cultivated in society.

***

Religion and science are neither competitors nor they are opponents.

Some questions of life religion cannot answer.

While some of them science cannot answer.

When both appear the quiz of life in individual capacity they become runner up. And when they appear as a team both becomes winner.

✳✳✳

Science cannot provide solace in death;
Religion cannot fulfill material needs.
Science cannot show which path is beneficial for man;
Religion cannot provide the material strength and energy required to walk on the path.
Both are incomplete in themselves.
Both are complete in co-ordination ...

✳✳✳

COMPARATIVE REVIEW OF SCIENCE AND RELIGION

Science	*Religion*
The ultimate truth of existence has not been discovered and will be discovered by future generations.	*The ultimate truth of existence has been discovered and was discovered by ancestors in the past.*
Search Knowledge in Future.	*Search Knowledge in Past.*
Implies that future generations will be more intelligent and knowledgeable.	*Implies that the previous generations were more intelligent and knowledgeable.*
Believes that material exists before consciousness.	*Believes that consciousness exists before material.*
The unity seen in different theories at the external level results in	*The diversity seen in different religions at the external level results in*

diversity at the subtle level. For example, the subtle motion of atoms cannot be explained by classical mechanics.	*unity at the subtle level. For example, despite different methods of worship, religion points to the same Supreme Power.*
Many experiential and experimental theories exist.	*Only one theory of karma, accepted by faith and inner self- exists.*
Many theories of Universe cannot be unified into a single theory. For example, the principles of gravity and atomic science cannot be combined into a single principle.	*Many aspects of religion, are combined into one principle. That is* *the retribution of the fruits of karma,*
principles that seems representing truths are at microscopic level, linguistic expressions of the experiences of scientists	*It is the linguistic expression of inner revelation of the saints and sages.*

✳✳✳

Even the phenomena of a small space and time of nature follows an unchanging and eternal principle. When this is realized, the study and faith in science are strengthened.

The entire universe-the entire existence in the form of infinite space and eternal time also follows an unchanging and eternal principle; when this is realized, the study and faith in religion are strengthened.

Therefore, the study and faith in science cannot make a student deviate from the study and faith in religion. The great scientists who believed in God and religion such as Galileo, Pascal, Newton, Einstein, Schrödinger, Oppenheimer, Heisenberg and Srinivasa Ramanujan, all show the same thing.

Similarly, it is equally true that the study and faith in religion cannot alienate a seeker from the study and faith in science, as Bacon, Leibnitz, Mendel, Aryabhata, Brahmagupta and Madhava, who worked in both the fields of religion and science, all show the same thing .

External observation of nature gives knowledge of the principles of science.

Internal observation of the conscience gives knowledge of the principles of religion.

The principles of science can describe only the small events of a fixed space-time period in coherent-logical principles . The same principles fail to understand those natural phenomena on a large scale, Therefore, science has to formulate other principles for events involving extremely large or minute dimensions.

Therefore, ultimately, science cannot understand the entire universe perfectly .

While religion is the science of moving from imperfection to perfection.

Logical and consistent steps of science :: Linguistics - Economics - Law - Political Science - Sociology – Philosophy - Psychology - Biology - Chemistry - Physics - Mathematics. Mathematics is the ultimate, logical and eternal truth of science.

Logical and consistent steps of religion :: Ethics - Worship - Rituals - Religious Work - Devotion - Good Deeds - Faith in the Supreme Soul - Knowledge and Worship - Yoga –Spiritual

Knowledge - Self Knowledge. Self Knowledge is the ultimate, logical and eternal truth of religion.

✱✱✱

4.2* RELIGION AND FAITH*

Religion is the faith received by a person from his parents in order to provide guidance in journey of life.
The faith is the religion invented by a person from guidance received from journey of life on its own.

✱✱✱

4.3* TRUTH AND GOD*

In the matter of truth and God; doubt those who have found.
Trust those seekers who are still in search of them.
And never follow any one and only one in total.

✱✱✱

4.4*RELIGION AND LANGUAGE*

Understanding of your own remains incomplete unless you learn others.

✱✱✱

4.5* GOD THE MASTER MATHEMATICIAN*

When you do some mathematics, and when you do some mathematical analysis,realize some beautiful truth or came to know some marvelous harmony or symmetry, you realize that you are not the first person to do this or to realize this. Somebody else has already realized this or somebody has already recognized the mathematical truth prior to you. And that somebody is nobody else but almighty God. God is the master Mathematician.
God has realized all the mathematical truths before we all have borne.

***

4.6*LIFE IS LIKE A TEXTBOOK OF MATHEMATICS*

Life is like a textbook of Mathematics. where every chapter ends in problems but answers are available at the end.
Where if understanding of fundamental is lacking, the problems cannot be solved on your own.
Where if any intermediate step is missed, the journey ahead becomes difficult.
Where if you love reading it, it reveals to you it's amazing inherent beauty

***

4.7* MATHEMATICS AND TIME*

Time is abstract;
Mathematics too is abstract .
Time is infinite;
Mathematics too is infinite.
Time has three phases, Past, Present and Future;
Mathematics too has three types of Numbers. Negative, Zero and Positive .
Time is measured by cyclic computations of frequencies and rotations enormously ;
Mathematics too has enormous process of cyclic computations.
That is why in Srimad Bhagvad Gita Lord Krishna Says to Arjun-
That- " I am the Time among those who are computing "

***

4.8* MATHEMATICS IS LIKE*

Structure of mathematics is like a brain, where each neuron is connected with another neuron in complex interconnected web of synapses. In which all neurons has a specific path of connection with each one of them.

Mathematics too has a complex web of interconnected mathematical truth. Where each mathematical truth cannot go against any another mathematical truth, as each one is interconnected with each other. All mathematical truths can only affirm the another one. Hence many a time an interconnection is being found between two different fields of Mathematics, believed to be isolated and seems to have no relation between them. Such fields seeming distinct are unified in single mathematical field. One such example is Rene Descarte's unification of Algebra and Geometry in the 17th Century.

✷✷✷

4.9* IN THE WORLD OF MATHEMATICS*

When you arrive at the result after some computation;
You feel that you are not the alone and came to this result for the first time;
Somebody else has already done this computation and he knows the result.
You are simply required to match your result with the already known result.
If your result matched with already known result then result is true or else your result is false.
There exists universal super computer and it has already performed all possible computations before anybody else and all the results are known to it.
That Universal super computer is nobody else but the almighty GOD.
GOD is the Master Mathematician and all computations and results are known to him prior to anybody else ...
If you deeply immerse in the immense and infinite world of the Mathematics and see the beauty of patterns and symmetry you

cannot be remain an atheist ; but you transforms yourselves in devotee of infinite, and doing mathematics becomes your prayer for the GOD.

***

4.10* MATHEMATICS AND MUSIC*

There is one faculty of science deeply rooted in pattern, rhythm, symmetry and harmony, with its infinite manifestation and that is the mathematics. There is one faculty of arts deeply rooted in pattern rhythm, symmetry and harmony with its infinite manifestations and that is the music.

If you are pondering on the solution of a difficult mathematical problem and you do not reach near any clue.

Listen the melodious and beautiful symphony of music and meditate on the problem simultaneously.

At the end when silence prevails the echoes of the music reverberates in your mind. Seat silently. And probably you may have a clue striking suddenly in your mind.

The very reason is that the Mathematics and music are deeply rooted in each other.

Because the secret codes of the patterns of mathematics cannot be decoded by the brain unless your heart has earlier decoded the secrets of similar patterns in the form of music.

***

4.11*ONE TIME – ONE GOD*

In our dreams, we flow in different times. When we awake, our dreams are broken and we flow in
one universal time.
In the similar manner –
When we are in the deep sleep of ignorance, we believe in different Gods. When we awake, our illusion is broken and we believe in one God.

✳✳✳

4.12*THE PRINCIPLE PRIME NUMBERS 1,2,3,5,7,11*

In the world of Mathematics, Prime numbers are considered as building blocks. Out of all, first six prime numbers are the most important, amazing and divine. They are primary building blocks of foundation of Mathematics. They are governing and limiting many aspects of Mathematics, Geometry, Physics, Cosmology, Nature and World. These numbers too appear repeatedly in Spirituality, Religion and Philosophy as well....

1=GOD PRIME= Formless but take all the forms. Number one is inherently attached with every number as the multiple of each number. God too is present in every form existing in nature.

2=MOTHER PRIME= The only Even prime number and it symmetrically splits in two parts.Giving birth and getting split in two parts is a quality of mother too. Hence number two is like Mother Giving Birth to all other number forms. Every Prime number appears as a factor of the form $2^n\pm1$which is a union of number two and one.

3=SPACE TIME PRIME= The space and time are deeply governed by number three. Space has three axis x,y and z. Time has three phases past, present and future. Space and nature split themselves in three dimensions. There are only three subatomic particles, Electron, Neutron and Proton. They are further comprising of three subatomic particles Quarks, Bosons and Leptons.

5= BODY PRIME= Every living form- having body is deeply governed by number five. Body has five senses Sight, Sound, Smell, Taste, and Touch.All naturalphysical bodies are comprising of five elements, space, wind, earth, fire and water.

7=NATURE PRIME = Nature is amazingly governed by number seven as limiting number. There are only seven colors

Violet, Indigo, Blue, Green, Yellow, Orange and Red. There are only seven musical knots Sa, Re, Ga, Ma, Pa, Dha and Ni. Natural Elements too follow this limit in periodic table in chemistry it too has seven rows of seven. Also, in week too has seven days as days repeat after seven days.

11= COSMIC PRIME = In string theory in cosmology, and in standard model of universe all symmetries can fit- if the universe model is considered to have eleven dimensions. Eleven is the ultimate limit of symmetries in cosmos.

✳✳✳

4.13* MATHEMATICS AS A MANIFESTATION OF GOD*

One of the Attribute of God is infinite (Om Purnmadh purnmindam ॐ पूर्णमद: पूर्णमिदम)

One of the Attribute of God is nullum(Neti Neti नेति नेति)

One of the attribute of Mathematics is Infinity(∞)

One of the attribute of Mathematics is zero (0)

Mathematics is a no ordinary science ,

It is a manifestation of God …

As God has written Secret code of creation in Mathematics …

As God remains unknown to us …

Some of the mysteries of Mathematics will going to remain ever unknown to us ..

$1/0=\infty, 1/\infty=0, 0/\infty=0, \infty/0=\infty, 0^{\infty}=0, \infty^{\infty}=\infty$

$\infty+\infty=\infty \quad \infty*\infty=\infty$

$0/0=?, \infty-\infty=? \quad \infty/\infty=? \quad 0*\infty=?, \quad 0^0=1 \ or \ ?, \quad \infty^0=?, \quad 1^{\infty}=?$

✳✳✳

4.14*IF YOU FEAR THE SUBJECT OF MATHEMATICS*

If you do not like and love to do the Mathematics …

If you are not able to appreciate the inherent beauty of the subject of Mathematics …

Then perhaps you are not blessed, and have not met a teacher of Mathematics who himself like and love to do the Mathematics,

64

who can introduce to you the inherent beauty of Mathematics and who can remove your fear of mathematics ...

✳✳✳

4.15*MATHEMATICAL TRUTHS*

An Equation is nothing to me unless it expresses a thought of God – Srinivasa Ramanujan

The most complex truths of mathematics are closely and deeply related to the simplest truths of mathematics.

Any single truth of mathematics is coherently and consistently connected with many other truths of mathematics. Therefore, no single truth of mathematics can be contradicted by other truths of mathematics.

The components of mathematics like numbers-figures-set, are connected with other components by the concept of the God, Formula is the mathematical expression of that connection conceptualized by the God.

The knower of the infinite calculation of mathematics is the God.

You cannot obtain any calculation result of mathematical calculation whose calculation result has not been calculated by the God before.

And hence the invention of any new calculation is not possible in the world of mathematical calculation.

Only the recollection of the mathematical result as per what has been calculated by the God is possible.

✳✳✳

4.16*GOLD MINE COAL MINE*

Those who are staunch supporters of religious scriptures and who are considering nothing but only gold mine , they should understand that when you move plenty of earth mass in goldfield you find small nugget of gold .

Those who are strong opponents of the religious scripture and who are considering it as nothing but only coal mine ,they too should understand that when you mine plenty of earth mass in coalfield you find diamonds

If you are hard working and skilled miner with passion and patience to mine plenty of earth mass you will sure get the glittering golden nuggets and precious diamonds ate greater depth of mine

***

4.17*NO BODY KNOWS*

No body knows Geometry , Numbers ,Patterns and colours better than leaves and flowers

***

4.18*MATHEMATICS IS A LANGUAGE TOO

IF YOU CAN SEE*

Digits, Algebric variables and constants, Geometric element such as point ,line and plane all these as alphabets.

Numbers, monomials and geometrical figures as words.

Grammar as Rules and laws .

Punctuations as symbols.

Prime numbers as Vowels.

Composite numbers as constants .

Geometry as script.

Polynomial, expression or statement as sentence .

Equation as interrogative sentence .

Identity as declarative or assertive sentence.

Formula as verses.. Theorems as prose..

Logic of elegant proof as poetry.

Algorithm as stanza. Tables as dictionary .

Thumb rules and postulates as sayings and proverbs .

Calculation and derivation as story and tale .

Final result as concluding morale of story .
Steps in derivation as paragraphs .
Area division or branches as epic.
Geometric construction as calligraphy .

****

4.19 *ATHEIST AND BELIEVER *

The atheist says: Man is the image of God, created in the same face,shape and form as himself.
While the believer says: God created the image of man in the same face, shape and form as himself......

****

4.20*THE STAGES OF SPIRITUAL EVOLUTION *

According to the Spiritual Philosophy and vision of the Sanatana - Hindu Religions sacred scripture, the final stages of spiritual evolution are as follows :

1.Nostalgia,Melancholia,Grief,Sadness   (Vishad-विषाद)—Over all observation of the world and the vision of its vanity, impermanence, despair and discouragement – it is borne out of being too much involved in the world

2.Dispassion, Detachment (Vairagya-वैराग्य)-Absence from worldly objects and their renunciation is Vairagya, it is born from Nostalgia, vishad .

3Liberation, Emnacipation, (virakti-विरक्ति)-means withdrawal from attachment or desire and it is born from vairagya.

4.Salvation,Emancipation(Vimukti विमुक्ति-Moksha-मोक्ष)-The state of liberation from all bondages, attachment, world and Maya, it is born from virakti . That is the final stage of liberation and the stage of salvation, emancipation, vimukti , moksha, nirvana or   kaivalya. This ultimate stage of achievement is the supreme being is pranav ॐ   OM- is the literal manifestation of parabrahma(परब्रह्म) *– supreme being or supreme truth.*

✳✳✳

4.21*THE SPIRITUAL INTERPRETATION OF EULER'S FORMULA *

When you see the beauty of Euler's identity $e^{i\pi}+1=0$ you will realise the truth behind the quotation of Srinivasa Ramanujan "An equation is nothing to me unless it expresses a thought of God

e=Exponential Growth=Ego

i=imaginary, illusion =maya

π=Ratio of perimeter of Circle to diameter also representing perimeter =Samsar Chakra =Wheel of Life

+=Added to in Association with=In presence of

1=Unity=God

= = Equal to =Attained to

0=Zero=Existence of nothing =Moksha

Ego of Soul increased under influence of Maya keeps soul moving in Samsara Chakra When it comes in devotional association with God, it attains moksha

This may be perhaps a thought of God expressed in this formula . All other civilisation failed to invent Zero. Only India succeeded in inventing Zero .The very reason behind is that the ultimate Goal of seeker of truth in India is nothing but the moksha .

✳✳✳

4.22 *INFINITE ATTRIBUTES OF GURU *

सब धरती कागद करूँ लेखनि सब वनराई।
सात समुद्र की मसी करूँ गुरु गुन लिखा न जाई ॥
- संत कबीर

Sab Dharti Kagad Karun lekhani sab vanrai
Saat samudra ki masi karun guru gun likha n jai
- Saint Kabir

Even if I take entire earth as paper, all forestry as pen, ink of all seven seas the attributes of Guru cannot be written.

This is the meaning of couplets from saint kabir, where the meaning of गुरु *guru is spiritual teacher, saheb or supreme master, God or Supreme Being...where meaning of* गुण *gun is attributes, qualities,properties or characteristics*

The existence of Supreme being is infinite and omnipresent. That supreme being manifest in its infinite forms and colors. That supreme being has many attributes or qualities which can be understood by man. That supreme being or ultimate truth is God . God is also named or in the form of Parmeshwar that is supreme existence pervading all cosmos. God is also in the form of Govind- Shri Krishna. That God is revealed to us by spiritual master, teacher or guru. To write attribute papers, pen and ink are required. To write the attributes of the eternal existence the guru, grains of soil are spread infinitely on the earth. This are the letters of prayers of the explanation of attributes of the guru. This are written on the earth by the pen of all forestry-trees with the ink of immense water of oceans. This is a analogy for infinity. That guru is a form of knowledge, peace and joy. This guru is also all pervading, all powerful and all knowing. This guru is manifested through art and beauty and is being expressed by the language. The very same infinity is present everywhere. This existence is shining with all its vastness and universality. Even the infinite letters cannot describe the attributes of guru in totality. knowledge of all books is also pointing towards that only. Millions of books written on different subjects is descriptions of divine attributes of that supreme existence, that description is still incomplete. The every atom of all cosmos becomes one word each and energy keeping them dancing becomes the grammar- with such a language the attributes, glory and praise of guru is infinitely, self-narrated eternally .

✱✱✱

4.23 *INDIA IS BHARAT MATA *

India is not merely a geopolitical boundary, hence it is not only a country, but in its essence it is something more than that;
India is not merely about the customs, values, traditions and art hence it is not only a culture, but in its essence it is something more than that;
India is not merely aggregation of people of common descent, history, language and state hence it is not only a nation, but in its essence it is something more than that;
India is not merely about people who have attained very advanced level of culture, art , commerce and governance of state hence it is not only civilization, but in its essence it is something more than that;
India is not merely about people who have a particular system of faith, belief, and worship hence it is not only a religion, but in its essence, it is something more than that;
India is an eternal, ever-transforming, and reforming humane quest, for the spiritual interpretation of life, nature, soul, ultimate truth, and God ...
India is the mother Goddess, Bharat Mata ...Ever caring and nourishing Mother ... Bharat mata ki Jai ...Vande Mataram .. Jai Hind .

***

4.24*AT THE END OF SERMON OF SRIMAD BHAGVAD GITA *

At the end of sermon of Srimad Bhagvad Gita, Speech of Lord Shri Krishna,As Lord Shri Krishna is completely free from any will, unattached and dispassionate in his sermon to Arjuna so he says that-)

यथेच्छसि तथा कुरु

Yathechhcasi tathaa kuru.

Do act as per your understanding and desire.

Arjuna's response in the end part of the sermon of the srimad bhagvad Gita

(Arjuna, having lost his attachment and delusion, after listening to the sermon of the Srimad Bhagvad Gita and having regained the memory of knowledge,   says to Lord Shri Krishna   with faith, dedication and surrender)

नष्टो मोहः स्मृतिर्लब्धा

करिष्ये वचनं तव

Nashto moha smrutirlabdhaa, karishye vachanm tav.

My attachment and delusion has ended and I have regained memories of my knowledge, hence I will act according to your sermon.

In the last part of the sermon of the Srimad Bhagvad Gita, After listening to the entire sermon of Srimad Bhagvad Gita, Sanjay (Who was charioteer of king Dhritrashtra — who was blessed to have divine vision (by Maharshi Ved Vyas to see war of the Mahabharat and to narrate it to king Dhritrashtra) can clearly see the outcome of the Mahabharata war and conveys his opinion to Maharaj Dhritarashtra as -

यत्र योगेश्वरः कृष्णो यत्र पार्थो धनुर्धरः।

तत्र श्रीर्विजयो भूतिर्ध्रुवा नीतिर्मतिर्मम॥

Yatra yogesgvarh krushno yatra partho dhanurdharh.

Tatr shreervijayo bhutitrdhruva neeteermatirmam.

It is my belief and opinion that - where there is Yogeshvar (God in deep meditation) Shri Krishna and the archer Arjuna are present, there is victory, immense wealth, divine manifestations of godly power, and unwavering leadership.

CHAPTER-5
THE PATH THAT READER FOLLOWS

5.1* THE BEGINNING*

Many will say : I have no time to read ;
Those who do not want to read will say,
I will read at proper time ;
Those who want to read will make time proper to read .
Those who do not want to read will say I will read at some time ;
Those who want to read will sum their,
 time and reading ;
Those who say now will be enriched, awakened and enlightened.

***

5.2*THE PURPOSE*

Many read to pass time;
A few read to understand how the time can be passed.
Many like to read. A few read to understand which thing to be
liked. Many reads to learn. A few learn how to read .

***

5.3* THE BOOKS*

Everybody talks about book !
Majority of them only looks at the book ;
Many of them simply open the book ;
Some of them read the book;
A few of them understand the book ;
Rarest of them put the content of the book in to the action.

***

5.4* THE DICTIONARY*

Many things look fractured, heterogeneous and random if you will read without the help of dictionary.

Everything becomes synthesized, homogeneous and proper if you read with the help of dictionary.

***

5.5* THE NUMBERS*

If you read ;
One book on the subject you will be left with more questions and less understanding.
Two books on the subject you will be left with some questions and some understanding.
More book on the subject less questions and more understanding.
Many books on the subject questions vanish and understanding get perfected.
If you read -
One book on the subject you will understand definitions and formulas.
Two books on the subject you will start understanding laws and orders.
A few more books you will understand applications and synthesis.
Many books you will master the subject.

***

5.6* THE REPITIONS*

If you read :
Once you will forget soon;
Twice you will remember for some days ;
Thrice you can remember prolong;

If writing follows reading you can remember forever.

***

5.7* THE LANGUAGE*

If you read in-
One language you will understand the meaning of the word.
Two languages you will understand translation.
Three languages you will start understanding grammar.
More languages you will understand communication.

***

5.8* THE SUBJECTS*

If you read :
One subject you will consider it is distinct ,
Two subjects you will think it is different .
A few more subjects you will understand it is little different.
Many subjects you will realize that it is not different.

***

5.9* THE PERSONALITY*

Those who read :
Language becomes literate.
Art becomes artist.
Commerce becomes businessman.
Science becomes scientist.
Who integrates all becomes personality.

***

5.10*WHAT THE DIFFERENT PERSONS READ*

A poet reads in words and feelings.
An artist reads in visions, beauty and music.
A scientist reads in matter, motion, space and time.
A philosopher reads in mystery of nature

A saint reads in humanity and worship of God .
A businessman reads in wealth.
A hungry reads in food.
A miserable reads in compassion.
A needy read in help.
A courageous reads in truth and sacrifice.
A young reads in love .
An awakened reads within.

****

5,11*THE SUBJECTS (LANGUAGE)*

Many read language for reading, writing and speaking.
Some reads language to say something from heart.
A few reads the language for exploitation of capacity of mind with language.

****

5.12.*THE SUBJECTS (MATHEMATICS)*

Many read mathematics for calculating and measurement.
Some reads mathematics for formula theorem and proof.
A few reads mathematics for the exploitation of capacity of mind to understand - generalization, synthesis, order, arrangement and to think beyond counting, forms, shape and calculation.

****

5.13* THE SUBJECTS (ARTS)*

Many read and perform arts to show.
Some perform arts in search of pleasure and peace of mind.
A few share pleasure, peace and beauty of mind by performing arts.
Some sees beauty in nature,
A few see beauty in themselves.

✳✳✳

5.14*THE SUBJECTS (COMMERCE)*

Many read practice and consider commerce as a science of accumulating wealth.
Some understand conveyance of wealth is more powerful than accumulating wealth .
A few understand love is more powerful than wealth.

✳✳✳

5.15* THE SUBJECTS (SCIENCE)*

Many read and study science to understand principles. Rules, movements, power, energy,force and light.
Many study science to understand its application and utility.
Many study science for achieving comfort and power.
A few study sciences for understanding true harmony hidden in nature and by that true understanding to serve humanity.

✳✳✳

5.16* WHAT TO READ*

Read which is eternal and ageless.
Read which has come out of the pen of the seekers of the truth.
Read which has emerged as water from the fountainhead from the sufferings of the heart, wisdom of the mind, art of the life, love from the humanity, beauty of the nature and symphony of the eternal and ageless existence .Read which has wiped out the tears of crying eyes, given the solace to the sufferings and awakening to the ignorant.

✳✳✳

5.17* THE READING*

Many read books in library.
And many other reads in society ,

And many others read in nature,
And many other reads in living ,
A few reads without reading .

****

5.18* THE LOVE*

Many reads for just reading.
Many reads in sufferings.
Many reads to earn.
Some understands love after reading.
Rarest of them understand love before reading.

****

5.19*THE LIVING*

Many understands reading is living.
Some understand living is reading.
Rarest of them reads and understand living is leaving.

****

5.20*THE CULMINATION*

Many go on reading after reading.
Some starts living after reading.
A few share reading and living with others by love.
Many read in reading.
Some reads in living.
A few of them finds reading in living and living in reading.
Rarest of them reads living by leaving..

****

www.ingramcontent.com/pod-product-compliance
Lightning Source LLC
Chambersburg PA
CBHW040130150726
48005CB00015B/2438